poingo

START

Disney PRINCESS

Sleeping Beauty

A very long time ago, in a magical kingdom, a beautiful princess was born.

King Stefan and his queen proclaim a holiday to celebrate the birth of their only child.

Joyful crowds gather at the castle to wish the very best for the Princess Aurora.

The king's guests include the three good fairies, Flora,

Fauna, and Merryweather.

Each fairy will give the baby a single magical gift.

Flora goes to the cradle first. "Little princess, my gift shall be

the gift of beauty," she says.

Next, with a wave of her wand, Fauna gives the baby the gift of song.

Suddenly the evil fairy Maleficent appears!

Upset that she wasn't invited to the celebration, Maleficent puts a curse on the baby! Before sunset on her 16th birthday, the princess will cut her finger on the spindle of a spinning wheel and die. "Oh, no!" the Queen cries.

Luckily, Merryweather has not given her gift yet. The good fairy's gift is to change the curse as best as she can: If Aurora cuts her finger on a spindle, she will fall only into a deep sleep and awaken with True Love's Kiss.

Flora has an idea to protect Princess Aurora from the terrible curse. The three good fairies will turn themselves into peasant women and raise the baby, deep in the forest.

Merryweather wonders if they will have to feed the baby.

"And wash it and dress it and rock it to sleep!" Fauna exclaims happily.

The fairies take the baby to the forest and call her "Briar Rose."

Briar Rose grows up in a hidden cottage with her loving "aunts"—Flora, Fauna, and Merryweather. Her only friends are the animals in the woods.

On her 16th birthday, Briar Rose spends the day picking berries and singing a song about love.

Not far from Briar Rose, a prince named Phillip falls off his horse and into a stream. He hangs his cape and hat on a tree to dry.

Meanwhile, Briar Rose tells the animals about the prince she sees in her dreams. "He's tall and handsome and so romantic!" she says.

The animals spot Prince Phillip's clothes and have an idea to surprise Briar Rose. They take the clothes and dress up as a prince!

Prince Phillip follows the beautiful voice that sings of love.

He spots Briar Rose dancing with her pretend prince, and steps in to take the animals' place.

Suddenly Briar Rose realizes that she is dancing with a young man who is real! The two talk until Briar Rose remembers that her aunts said not to talk to strangers.

She runs off but agrees to meet the young man later that evening.

At the cottage, the fairies get ready to celebrate Briar Rose's 16th birthday.

Fauna makes the cake but isn't sure about the ingredients. She puts two eggs in the batter, shells and all! The cake looks rather funny.

Merryweather and Flora make Briar Rose a new dress, but the dress looks strange, too.

"Shhhh!" Fauna whispers when she hears Briar Rose coming back from the forest.

Just in time, the fairies use their magic wands to fix the dress and cake.

"This is the happiest day of my life!" exclaims Briar Rose. She tells the fairies that she just met the young man of her dreams.

The fairies realize that Briar Rose is in love! Finally they tell her who she really is: a princess named Aurora. That night, the fairies will take her back to her parents. The princess will not see the young man again.

"Oh, no, no!" Princess Aurora cries.

At the castle, King Stefan waits anxiously for his daughter with his friend, King Hubert.

After the princess was born, King Stefan had promised that his daughter would marry King Hubert's son, Prince Phillip. Finally the time has come for Princess Aurora to marry the prince!

King Hubert raises his glass. "To the future!" he says.

The Royal Wedding
the Court Jester
the Three Fairies
the Herald
the Knight
the Minstrel
the Noble

That evening, the fairies sneak back to the castle with Princess Aurora. When they leave the princess alone for a moment, Maleficent uses her evil magic! Under Maleficent's spell, Princess Aurora follows a glowing light to a spinning wheel. She touches the spindle and falls into a deep sleep.

The fairies are heartbroken but all is not lost. They discover that the young man whom the princess met in the forest was Prince Phillip. The prince could break the spell with True Love's Kiss!

Maleficent tries to stop Prince Phillip from reaching Princess Aurora. With the fairies' help, the prince rides through a forest of thorns and defeats Maleficent in a battle!

Finally, in the castle, the fairies lead Prince Phillip to his true love. He kneels next to Princess Aurora and gives her a gentle kiss.

With True Love's Kiss, the princess awakens!

Prince Phillip and Princess Aurora walk arm in arm to greet their happy parents. King Stefan and King Hubert can't believe their eyes!

The fairies watch the princess and Prince Phillip dance.

"Oh, I just love happy endings!" Fauna says, crying with happiness.

Finally the princess is with her true love, just the way she always dreamed.